THIS BOOK BELONGS TO

You, who found this book today.
Hope you enjoy the ride.
Love

Alousa Goudarzi

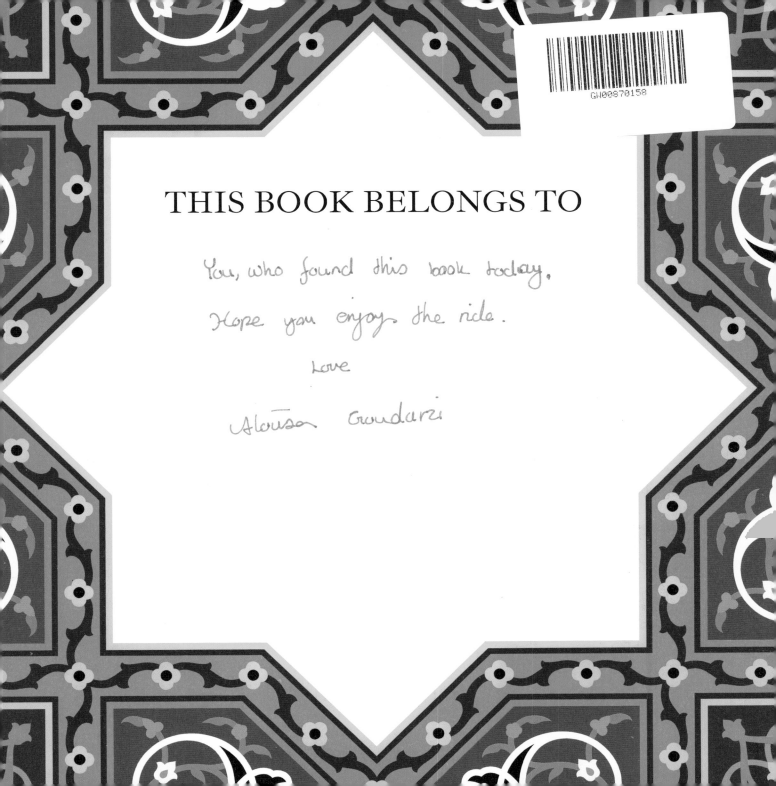

www.caspicaarthouse.com

ISBN: 9798353974789

To IR655,
which never got to cross
the Persian Gulf

PERSIA
AND THE
VALLEY OF GOLD

Written by Dr Atousa Goudarzi
Illustrated by Gabriela Issa Chacon

Once upon a time, in a land far away,
lay the richest and most beautiful
valley of all time.

To enter this valley, you must say
these magic words three times:
"Let's get ready and get steady!
Leaving behind our fear, already."

Welcome to the Valley of Gold,
the richest to ever exist. The valley is
surrounded by many beautiful countries.
Amazing animals frolic, and sunshine gleams
on sparkling sand in perfectly flat deserts.

North of this valley lies the prosperous city of Gor. This is a circular city said to have been built by enchanters. Gor is full of friendly, happy people and curious animals.

In the middle of this city stands a tall, beautiful tower, home to a nosy lizard named Voor Voor. He is a fast and clever lizard. But sometimes, Voor Voor gets into big trouble.

On this warm, spring day, Voor Voor rests at the peak of the tower. Suddenly, he notices a dark cloud appearing in the sky. It is not like any rain cloud he has ever seen. It is darker and bigger! It is moving extremely fast!

Voor Voor scurries to follow the dark cloud until it reaches the edge of Gor. Without warning, the dark cloud begins to drop huge boulders of gold onto Gor. In shock, the lizard sees one of them land right on top of a house!

Holding his breath, he watches a little girl crying for help outside the crushed door. She tries to move the boulder, but it is too heavy. Voor Voor hears voices coming from inside. "Persia! Are you all right? Do not worry about us! Your father and I are unharmed."

"I am okay, Mother. But I am very scared!" cries Persia.
"What shall I do about this boulder of gold that has fallen on
our home?"

A man's voice from inside shouts, "I know how scared you must be,
Persia. But stay strong! You can save us by finding a way to melt that gold.
Only then can we be freed. We have enough food and water for seven
days and seven nights," he assures. "We will wait for your return.
Remember, our love always stays with you."
Persia knows she must do something! She grabs her bag and walks
towards the Valley of Gold. Voor Voor decides to accompany
Persia and help her save Gor!

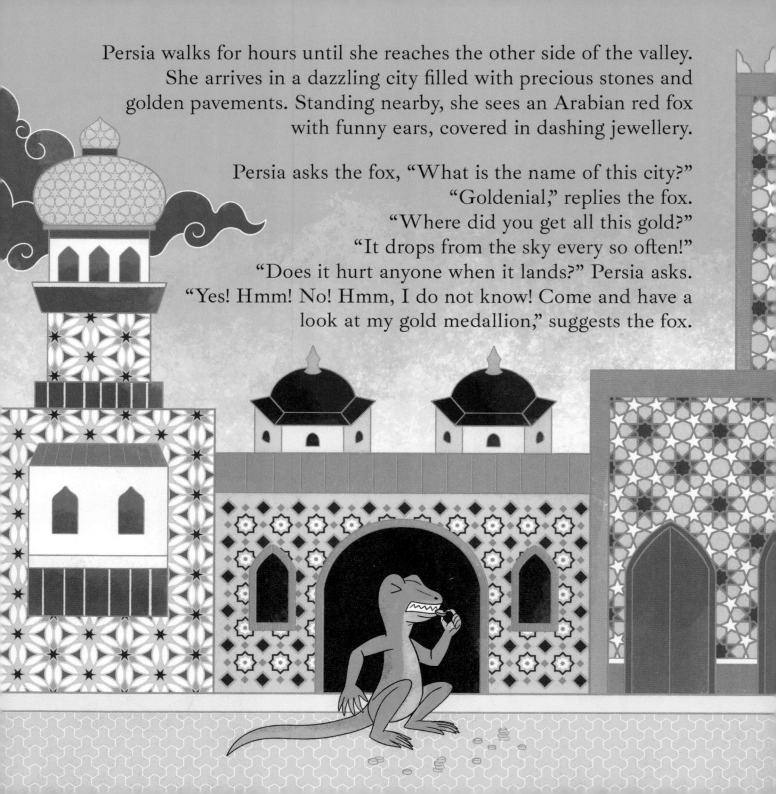

Persia walks for hours until she reaches the other side of the valley. She arrives in a dazzling city filled with precious stones and golden pavements. Standing nearby, she sees an Arabian red fox with funny ears, covered in dashing jewellery.

Persia asks the fox, "What is the name of this city?"
"Goldenial," replies the fox.
"Where did you get all this gold?"
"It drops from the sky every so often!"
"Does it hurt anyone when it lands?" Persia asks.
"Yes! Hmm! No! Hmm, I do not know! Come and have a look at my gold medallion," suggests the fox.

"Right now, we must find out why these boulders of gold are dropping on us!" says Persia. "We must stop it! This may be hurting many creatures."

The fox feels all hope is gone, and he says with a big yawn, "But what can I do? I am only ONE!"
"You are not the only ONE, I am here too.
One plus one will make us two," Persia replies.

They get ready and get steady.
Leaving behind their fear, already!

Persia and the fox walk in the silky desert for hours. They are tired and thirsty when they see Mount Ferwa. They decide to climb the mountain for a better view.

When they reach the top, they see a fast falcon flying in a strange pattern between Mount Ferwa and Mount Sawda. "Is she blind?" Persia wonders. "Why is she running into the rocks?"

Persia calls, "Do you need help? Your wings look broken and your beak is bleeding. Can you still see?"

"Have you not noticed the dark cloud
in the sky?" responds the falcon.
"It looks so scary and
keeps me from seeing clearly!"

"Yes, we have seen it, but you must take care
of yourself," says the fox. "Try not to be so anxious.
Sit down and breathe deeply. Face anything unknown
and scary by being calm and kind to yourself."

The falcon feels all hope is gone, and she says with a big yawn,
"But what can I do? I am only ONE!"
"You are not the only ONE, we are here, too, young and free.
One plus two will make us three," Persia replies.

They get ready and get steady.
Leaving behind their fear, already!

The trio heads towards the east. They soon see a loggerhead turtle digging large holes in the ground. "She does not need such big holes for her little eggs!" falcon suggests.

The turtle looks up and says, "Have you seen the size of the golden boulders the dark cloud drops? All this digging is making me tired, but I may have found how to bargain with it! I dig a big hole, and it leaves my eggs alone."

"You should not have to work this hard," says the falcon.
"Surely you can protect your eggs another way."

The turtle feels all hope is gone, and she says with a big yawn,
"But what can I do? I am only ONE!"
"You are not the only ONE, we are here, for sure. One plus
three will make us four," Persia replies.

They get ready and get steady.
Leaving behind their fear, already!

They carry on walking towards the sunrise and soon see a catlike caracal. The caracal is angrily tipping bags of sand onto the beach and planting palm trees.

The turtle asks, "What is the point in planting the trees, when you know they cannot spread their roots?"

"They make my place look pretty! I do not care that they last not long in the winds of the Shamal," replies the caracal in anger. "The dark cloud is making the wind even stronger! The Shamal is blowing all my beautiful sand AWAY. Where does the darkness come from? How can I get rid of it?"

The caracal feels all hope is gone, and he says with a big yawn, "But what can I do? I am only ONE!" "You are not the only ONE, together we thrive. One plus four will make us five," Persia replies.

They get ready and get steady. Leaving behind their fear, already!

The group now continues towards the sunset. Just before dark, on the fifth day of her journey, Persia notices an Arabian oryx with broken horns and many scars.

They walk to the oryx. The caracal says, "What has happened to you?"

The oryx hardly raises her head and says, "The boulders of gold keep falling from the sky. I cannot run fast enough to get away!"

The caracal whispers, "You might feel this is happening to only you and there is no end. I promise...this, too, shall pass." The oryx feels all hope is gone, and he says with a big yawn, "But what can I do? I am only ONE!"

"You are not the only ONE, we are a good mix. One plus five will make us six," Persia replies.

They get ready and get steady. Leaving behind their fear, already!

Persia has been away from home for six days and is no closer
to solving the mystery of the dark cloud and boulders of gold.
She is starting to lose hope. But when she looks at her new
friends, she finds strength to continue.

They keep moving towards the sunset when they see a little jerboa
running quickly back and forth. They stop him, and the oryx asks,
"Why are you running so fast?"

"Have you not heard the loud noise from
the valley? When I hear it, I start running.
I know that the heavy boulders of gold from
the sky will come next."

"What noise?" oryx asks.

"It sounds like thousands of eagles flapping their wings, hundreds of snakes hissing, and tens of elephants screaming," replies the jerboa.

"Have you tried to find out what makes those sounds?" Persia asks.
"No," answers the jerboa. But what can I do? I am only ONE!"
"You are not the only ONE. Think for a second!
One plus six will make us seven," Persia replies.

"Let's get ready and get steady.
Let's leave behind our fear, already!"

As they move onward to the valley on the seventh day, Persia is determined to solve the mystery of the dark cloud and save her parents.

When they arrive, they climb down into the valley for a better view. At the bottom, they find boulders of gold in the thousands! Surprisingly, they see people tying big chunks of meat to the large rocks.

Persia and her friends are full of questions. But they suddenly realise something has covered the sun. They look up and see a gigantic bird!

"Roc!" screams the falcon. "It is the great, elephant-eating bird of prey, with seven snake-like tongues."

Persia asks, "But what are all those people doing?"

Jerboa answers, "I see! The golden boulders are too heavy for people to carry up from the valley. When Roc tries to pick up the meat, the gold comes with it. Because the boulders are so heavy, they soon drop on the ground for people to collect."

The oryx says, "We must put a stop to this. So many lives are being damaged." Persia sits down to think. Just then, she notices Voor Voor holding a blue tiara.

"Avissa!" Persia cries. "Avissa can help us! Thank you, Voor Voor! Come on, everyone! We need a drop of sweat from each of you to bring Avissa to us. Gather around."

Persia and her friends make a circle and chant:
"We have crossed the desert to find peace, walked through the valley without ease. Here we are, you goddess of water, help us find peace in one another."
Their drops of sweat form a puddle. When Persia places the tiara in the puddle, Avissa appears!

Persia and her friends tell Avissa all about Roc and the Valley of Gold.

"Stand back!" Avissa cries. She uses her cane to melt the boulders of gold into a river of dark liquid that enters the earth. Now animals will no longer be harmed. She then uses another spell to fill the valley with turquoise blue water.

The clear, clean water magically becomes home to 700 different types of fish, shining pearls, and beautiful reefs.

Avissa then helps Persia cross the water to Gor, where her parents wait on the shore. Gor is once again a vibrant and happy city.

Everyone meets to bid Avissa farewell. Someone from the crowd asks, "What shall we name this beautiful gulf of water?"

Avissa looks into Persia's eyes. "I think we shall name it the 'PERSIAN GULF' for the bravery and care young Persia has shown in this place!"

Do you want to see the
Persian Gulf?
Ask a grown-up to show
you on your globe.

THE ANIMALS IN THE STORY

Arabian Red Fox

Did you know I have fur between my toes, to prevent burning of my feet when I run in a hot desert?

Peregrine Falcon

Did you know I am the fastest bird on the planet?

Loggerhead Turtle

Did you know with my powerful jaws, I can crush and munch on brittle ocean animals such as clams, crabs, and mussels?

Caracal
Did you know I can jump up to 3 meters (10 feet) into the air?

Arabian Oryx
Did you know I can detect rainfall and fresh plant growth from up to 90km (almost 56 miles) away?

Jerboa
Did you know I can leap up to 3 meters (10 feet)?

Printed in Great Britain
by Amazon

11095573R00022